# THE
# SHIFTY SERVANTS

## Maria Christine

A NOCTURNA PRESS BOOK

The Shifty Servants
First Edition, Second Printing
Copyright © 2020 Maria Christine

Nocturna Press
Independence, Missouri
www.NocturnaPress.com


ISBN-13: 978-1-944673-05-5 (paperback)
ISBN-13: 978-1-944673-04-8 (e-book)

ISBN-10: 1-944673-05-9 (paperback)
ISBN-10: 1-944673-04-0 (e-book)


Library of Congress Control Number: 2016914787

First printing November 2016

Published in the United States of America

*For women who rock*

# Chapter One

"Ah, the view of the castle is grand from here, isn't it, Ava?"

"Yes, Simone," Ava replied. "And it's so peaceful here in our spot under the trees."

A third woman, Cosette, suddenly stood in a panic. The three women had been taking a much-needed break from their duties serving the queen. "It's time to get back!" she cried. "Her majesty will have our heads!"

The women ran to the castle as fast as their cumbersome dresses would allow. They rushed to the castle past ovens stuffed with seasoned meats and chimneys billowing the smoky aroma of supper soon to be served. They hurried through a door to the hot kitchen filled with the pleasing scents of rye, honey, and sage.

Cosette grabbed her apron and threw it on quickly. "The ball is but hours from now. Not a thing must be out of place!" she warned the others.

"Yes, yes," Simone agreed. "Everything must be perfect!"

Mistress Ava darted out of the kitchen and swiftly up the staircase to prepare the queen's clothing.

Queen Geneva had a sizeable army, but a moderate troupe of servants. She trusted very few people and preferred to keep in her employ only what help was required to keep order. Of these, Simone, Cosette, and Ava were the most trusted in the queen's service. Cosette was head cook; Simone was head housemaid; and Ava was the queen's personal mistress-in-waiting. But they were also charged with keeping order amongst the lower-ranking domestics and with keeping her majesty abreast of the goings-on about the castle.

This was to be the night of the queen's ball, and the ruler of Dread Kingdom was the first and most important invited guest. Although the fearsome king's presence was recognized throughout the realm, it was not customary for him to make appearances. Unless, of course, it afforded him an opportunity to engage with the lovely Queen Geneva. Even the queen's three most trusted servants were not privy to certain details of their relationship. But the women firmly suspected that it was of a most romantic nature. And they were determined to find out for certain.

"Mistress!" The queen's powerful voice pierced the silent upstairs halls just as Ava hurried into her chambers.

"Yes, Your Majesty," she answered.

Queen Geneva turned around in her seat. Her brown hair was sculpted magnificently as always. Her rich, dark, skin and eyes were exotic and striking. She was quite beautiful, but a force to be reckoned with. "Oh, there you are," she said snidely. "Finally."

Ava walked into the queen's wardrobe and searched for the perfect evening gown and velvet slippers. The king has never seen her in this one, she remarked to herself. It was perfect.

"Yes, Mistress, you have done it again," said the queen. "It is marvelous! Red wine and gold. He will melt with desire."

Ava's eyes grew wide upon hearing that remark, but the queen didn't notice. The servant tightened her lips and smiled as she prepared the perfumes and oils for the queen's bath. She knocked a bottle to the floor, but Queen Geneva didn't notice that either. She stood at the mirror holding the dress up to herself and smiling seductively. Ava was tickled by this. She could hardly wait to speak with Simone and Cosette.

# Chapter Two

As the sun made its evening descent, the bard began to play, and guests to arrive. This night, the queen gave specific orders that her three chief servants pay particular attention to the needs of the king and his company. Dressed in their finest gowns, as was customary for all attending the queen's parties, Ava, Simone and Cosette anxiously awaited the arrival of the king and the Dread Knights.

"I hope there will be a fine young gentleman," said Simone, the younger of the trio.

"Even better to have three fine young gentlemen," Cosette corrected.

"I prefer mine a little bit older," said Ava. "Dark and distinguished, like a very fine wine." Her mind drifted away for several moments and upon return she noticed the eyes of the other two women fixed conspicuously upon her.

Cosette didn't blink, but raised a brow. Then Simone touched her arm. "Maybe we can get close enough to acquire some interesting information," she whispered.

"We're not courtesans," whispered Cosette. "How close do you expect us to get?"

"Close enough to glean any details about King Dominicus and our queen," said Simone with dreamy eyes. "I am certain it is a forbidden, whirlwind romance."

"You are such a romantic," said Cosette. "You read too much poetry."

"Possibly," said Simone. "But I just can't help it. The king is so dark and handsome, and the queen is beautiful and headstrong... I just know he is sweeping her off her feet."

"Well, I must be a romantic too, because I do agree," Cosette admitted, her voice lowering to even more of a whisper. "And the other royals and nobles are afraid of the formidable king. His wrath is legend. They avoid association with him at any cost. I believe that is the reason for her secrecy."

"Ah, yes," Simone sighed. "But love is love is love…"

Ava suddenly cleared her throat to alert the others of another's presence. "My lady," she said to the approaching woman with a gentle curtsy. She thought it strange that this particular woman would come to speak to them. "Is anything the matter?" asked Ava.

Cosette straightened her back. "Yes, Lady Hilda, may we be of service?"

Lady Hilda was a guest of noble blood. She'd been on previous visits to the castle, as it had been suggested to Queen Geneva that she would be a suitable lady-in-waiting. But Queen Geneva was never impressed by bloodlines and station. She surrounded herself with staff of her personal selection. The older woman felt slighted and made no secret of it from the younger ladies, who largely ignored her snide remarks and entitled manner. Hilda also felt a twinge of jealousy whenever she saw them. She begrudgingly admired Cosette's fair hair and eyes, and Simone's flawless skin and slenderness. But she equally admired Ava's more-shapely figure, warm tan complexion, and dark exotic features. It made her physically ill.

"Actually, I do have a reason for bothering with—" Hilda deliberately swallowed before continuing, "the likes of you."

Ava and Simone tried to conceal their dismay at the insult, but Cosette glared patently at the woman.

Hilda smirked proudly, "I want to warn you about the knights of Dread," she said. "They are accustomed to women of class and sophistication attending to their needs. One hopes they will not be disappointed when they arrive. The knights of Dread are quite infamously ill-tempered."

Cosette was imploding inside and Hilda knew it. She grinned satisfactorily and sauntered away.

Ava and Simone held Cosette back. She was moments from going after the woman when the musicians suddenly halted their song. An announcement was made of the arrival of King Dominicus.

The ruler of Dread Kingdom, dressed regally in black silk and velvet, was foreboding and marvelous. His skin was ivory. His hair was long and dark and several strands glistened like threads of pure silver. His eyes, piercing gray pools, were fixed on the queen. As the crowd parted, the king moved toward her.

Ava, Simone and Cosette noticed his provocative and flirtatious grin. And they weren't alone. His menacing, yet alluring presence unintentionally seduced every woman within sight of him.

Queen Geneva rose from the throne and walked gingerly down the carpeted staircase to greet the great king. As she stood before him, the three servants took careful note of their every move. The queen and king stared at each other for several moments. Then he took her hand to his lips. Everyone else kneeled and bowed. His eyes never left hers for a moment.

Ava whispered quietly to her cohorts, "Brilliant."

They nodded silently in agreement.

King Dominicus then escorted her majesty to the courtyard where the ball would officially begin. The music resumed.

Simone turned to Ava and Cosette. "Until they left, I couldn't draw a single breath!"

"Nor could I," said Cosette.

Ava was a bit flushed as her eyes followed the couple. "He is a beautiful king—*isn't he?*"

"Hush—" the others warned.

A tall, dark, shadow fell over Ava.

"I see you have quite an interest in my brother and your queen," said a man.

Ava turned quickly and curtsied before Prince Alucio. "Your Highness," she said with more urgency than she'd meant to.

He smiled and placed his hand gently under her chin, guiding her back up to him. "You needn't bow to me, dear lady," he said before kissing her hand.

She did not hear him at first because she was taken by his striking eyes and soft pouting lips. "My deepest apologies, Your Highness, I didn't mean to stare—I've forgotten my place."

"Calm, sweet woman. And you don't have to call me Your Highness, either," he grinned.

"But Your–" She stopped herself before continuing. "I am but a servant. I have no place…"

"And I am but a man," he insisted. "And I wish you would address me less formally."

"But the king…" she worried aloud.

"I am not the king," said Alucio. "And he does not dictate who I should and should not speak to. Do you understand?"

The way his lips curved into a winsome grin spoke to Ava with even more persuasion than his words. "Yes," she said.

"Good. Then say you'll join me for a stroll," he said politely.

"But my instructions are to attend to the needs of the king," she said.

Alucio sighed and took her hand. "Trust me when I say that the king's needs are quite met, and that it would benefit him greatly if he was left alone to enjoy them."

She understood his meaning. And after all, she and the others had also been instructed to attend the king's company. She would hesitate no more.

As mistress Ava left with her arm linked to his, her two comrades watched. They stood at their places in view of the king and queen but glared wickedly at Ava.

"How dare she leave us?" Cosette huffed.

Simone's eyes narrowed. "She left without a single word to us! And what does she think she's doing with the prince?"

"I knew we could never trust her," said Cosette. "Leaving us to work while she flirts shamelessly with the king's brother."

When they turned around and were immediately greeted by two of the king's knights, Sir Lazander and Sir Erec. For the first time in their lives, they were speechless—until the men asked them to dance. Simone eagerly accepted the request of Sir Erec and she hurried him to the dance floor. But Cosette was a little more reserved. "Well, one dance would be all right, I suppose. Yes," she said plainly.

Sir Lazander bowed to her with a perceptive grin and took her hand.

# Chapter Three

Ava and Prince Alucio took a long walk along the stream and through the gardens. They spoke of the weather and of their shared thoughts on the cosmos and the world around them. They spoke of their pasts, the present, and what they hoped for the future.

Eventually their path led them into the woods. They arrived at a beautiful glen with stone benches and a fountain in the center. Ava felt comfortable with Alucio, but there was still a part of her that warned against this lengthy time alone.

She worried not of him, but of judgment by her queen. The prince sensed this.

He led her to a bench and they watched as bluebirds drank from the fountain. "You've no reason to be nervous," said the prince. "I must let you in on a secret. My brother is madly in love with your queen, and she is in love with him."

Ava was taken aback by his sudden disclosure. She laughed to herself.

"You knew this?" asked Alucio.

"I suspected," said Ava with a smile.

"Dominicus does not care what the self-absorbed nobles think or say. Regardless of their station, most of them are the lowest of the low in terms of humanity. He is discreet because the queen wishes it."

Ava began to realize that the stories of the House of Dread were probably more speculation than fact. The king and his brother seemed less sinister than the legends had portrayed. But she was still certain that broadmindedness should not be mistaken for patience or weakness. "That is quite chivalrous of His Highness," she said. "And beautiful." She stood and continued along the path. Alucio followed.

"I do not suppose many men would be as understanding," said Ava.

Alucio walked with his hands held comfortably behind his back. "The men of our family have always been loyal and understanding of our women," he said.

Ava stopped and turned to him as he spoke.

"Women are fascinating and passionate creatures," he said, "and we do not take their love for granted."

Alucio placed his hands on either side of her face and looked on her gently as if memorizing her eyes. She relaxed into his caress and closed her eyes wantonly. He then kissed her sweetly on the lips, and then slowly broke away. "I am sorry, Ava. I had no right to do that."

She'd wanted his kiss, but she could see that the prince was genuinely embarrassed. She had to do something. So, she turned her back to him. "It's not your fault," she said dramatically. "It's a curse."

He was puzzled. "What do you mean?" he asked, placing a hand on her shoulder.

She turned to face him. "My beauty," she said. "It's a wonder you've resisted so long." She said this with such seriousness that he was momentarily stammered.

Suddenly she began to laugh and he realized that she'd been facetious in order to set him more at ease. He smiled. "Ava, you are truly remarkable. But never doubt your beauty. I have never desired a woman more."

Ava knew that if she ever committed her virtue, it would be to this man. And it was getting exceedingly difficult to resist his charms. To his surprise, she hiked her dress and stepped up onto a stone bench. Then she pulled the tall man closer. She took his head into her hands and kissed him back, and with such urgency that could only lead to much more. He gladly accepted this offering and then moved his mouth to her neck, tasting her, exciting her. She began to burn with desire. She closed her eyes and moaned softly, whispering into the wind, "heaven help me."

"Geneva."

"Yes, Dominicus?"

"Do you think that any one knows about us yet?"

"Oh my, yes," she said quietly. "My three most loyal servants have an idea and are falling all over themselves to find out the truth."

"I wonder where they are, anyway. They have been assigned to serve you tonight," she said.

He laughed. "I suspect they are attending my company. My brother and knights noticed them immediately as we arrived."

"But they are servants," said the queen.

"And who are we to judge the love of another?" he asked.

The queen agreed. "You are right, my loving king."

"Loving is a term only used by you to describe me," he said.

"Because only I see the truth," said Geneva. "If everyone else would only be kinder instead of provoking you, they too would see what I see."

"Are you trying to charm me?" he asked.

"Is it working?" she replied.

"Better than you might think," he said.

# Chapter Four

Darkness had fallen and a full moon was high. It had been a joyful night. Guests had enjoyed music, dancing, and a terrific supper. Soon it was time for the queen's favorite game, the passing of the rose. The game took place in the courtyard, which was decorated with thousands of roses and lit by torches. The unmarried women and the most eligible bachelors, apart from the king, were to participate. Each woman was given a rose of a different color. The men, including the prince of Dread Kingdom, were to choose a rose, while blindfolded, and then remove the blindfold and choose any lady whose rose matched the color of his own. The couple would be dance partners for the remainder of the evening.

Simone was delighted when Sir Erec chose a rose that matched her own and then chose her as his partner. Cosette was also as fortunate, but Ava was not. Her rose was red, and Prince Alucio had chosen yellow. He shot her a sad glance and she smiled to herself. But then he gave her a wink that told her he was up to something mischievous. He went to a certain lady whose rose matched his own while Ava looked on. He stood behind the woman and brought his hand around to her front, offering her the rose in a romantic fashion. "May I have this dance, Lady Hilda?" said the prince.

The older lady smiled wide. She was thrilled that she had been chosen by one of the handsome bachelors. But when she turned to see the fearsome prince, she couldn't contain her shock and let out an obvious yelp. She covered her mouth as if she could retract the noise, and he grinned roguishly. As afraid as she was, she had no choice but to dance with the prince, and he would thoroughly enjoy taking advantage of her plight. The older woman blushed terribly as he dipped her much as he would a lover, and whispered something wicked in her ear. Ava, the other servants, and even the king and queen took noticeable pleasure in Hilda's apparent unease.

Throughout the night, as Ava danced with a young, would-be suitor, she and Alucio shared many affectionate gazes, and Alucio even playfully shot menacing looks at her dance partner which humored her tremendously. The young man, who never noticed the prince's threatening glares, had occasion to ask her what was making her giggle. She simply said she was having the time of her life.

At the evening's close, the other guests had gone, and the women said woeful goodbyes to the men of Dread Kingdom. Prince Alucio kissed Ava's hand and said softly, "I would see you again, if you'll let me."

"As soon as fate allows, Your Highness," said Ava with a smile.

Prince Alucio gave her a sideways look and a grin. Her return to formality was due to the presence of the queen and king. Reluctantly, he turned to leave.

But before the king and prince could exit, a message was delivered hurriedly to the king. "It is most urgent, Your Majesty," said the kneeling messenger.

King Dominicus began to read the letter. His eyes became dark, but his look was otherwise emotionless. The servants became nervous, but the king said nothing. He then smiled at the queen and nodded his head as a second farewell. As the men took their leave, the mood was unsettling and cold. All of the women were left quite troubled.

## Chapter Five

At the castle of Dread, the troubled ruler and his brother pondered the situation in the library.

"Servants, leave us," said the king. He waved his hand to rush them from his presence, but his eyes never left the burning fireplace. "Alucio," he said.

"Yes, brother," Alucio replied.

"You realize this may mean war," said Dominicus.

"Yes."

Dominicus took a deep breath and clenched his teeth. "So, self-proclaiming himself as king is not enough for the Prince of Aldren. He has set his sights on my land now as well? Is that it?" he asked and turned to his brother. "Well, I want something from him as well," he said coldly. "I want his blood."

"And that you shall have, brother," said the prince. "That you shall have."

"But first," Dominicus snarled, "how did one of his men get close enough to the castle to even deliver the threat?"

"I have pondered that myself," said Alucio. "I suspect that someone here is working for him."

Dominicus took a sword from the wall and ran his thumb along the blade. "If that is the case, we're going to find out whom. And when we do, I want his head as a centerpiece in the dining hall. It will remind them the consequence of betraying me."

"As you wish, my brother."


A fierce clash of thunder quaked the land. Queen Geneva gazed into the stormy midnight sky from a window in the den.

"Your majesty! Your majesty!" Ava said anxiously as she rushed into the room. "This was just delivered and it bears the royal seal of Dread. I was informed that it is of utmost urgency and that I should hand-deliver to you without delay!"

The queen was very concerned as she opened the envelope. She'd been troubled for weeks because of the fighting at the boundaries of Dread Kingdom. Receiving an urgent message was quite worrying.

Prince Ethan of Aldren and his men were no match for the Dread Knights who were the most feared soldiers known on the continent. Any of the few who dared cross the king met a most painful demise. But because of a personal vendetta, the king himself had suited up and gone into the battle. The prince of Aldren had violently seized the smaller kingdoms lying outside the kingdom of Dread and had forced men from all of those regions to join his army upon penalty of death. He had amassed a large army and has promised the king's death. Ethan had become rather bold in his ambitions and many felt he had quite a death wish.

When Geneva finished reading the letter, she turned to her humble servant with a stern order. "Prepare for your departure," she commanded.

"Instruct Mistresses Cosette and Simone to do the same." The queen then turned her back to the servant and returned to the window in attempt to conceal any emotion. "You will be transported to Dread to care for a very wounded king."

# Chapter Six

Ava, Simone and Cosette rode in a carriage making way to Dread Kingdom. The hooves of the horses clopped loudly against the rocks and dirt, and the thunderous storm around them had not yet quelled.

Each woman had many questions, and their imaginations began to get the better of them.

"I'm nervous," whispered Simone. "We've never been to Dread Kingdom. I heard it is a very dark place."

"Yes," said Ava. "But we have our orders. The king needs us, as he is unsure who to trust."

"Do not worry," said Cosette. "We'll simply stick to our duties and blend in."

"Blend?" said Simone. "I heard that the servants are cold and unfeeling. And I heard that they dress in all black, and they have black eyes and gray skin, and never speak."

Ava nodded. "That is true. And I heard that the entire castle is engulfed in cobwebs, and that at night you are wakened by the high-pitched screams of innocent victims as they are tortured to their deaths."

Simone's eyes became very large. Thunder clashed, and all of the women jumped in their seats.

As they caught their breaths, Simone clutched her pocket bag tightly. She wasn't listening to anything the other women had said. She'd been in a daze of thoughts. "What if the king is not all right?"

"What are you saying, Simone?" asked Cosette. "That the king will die?"

Thunder clashed again. Cosette became nervous and Ava just looked on.

"It's only that he's hurt so badly," said Simone worriedly. "What if he dies while we're taking care of–" She choked back her words as fear overcame her.

Ava sighed. "Simone, you're worried about the consequences of his death at our hands?"

Simone looked up and nodded a profound and terrified yes.

Cosette was even more worried now at the mere thought. "That's ridiculous," she said. "It would not be our fault. We'll take very good care of him. And, and…" she stuttered, "And he will live anyway, so stop worrying about it!" She tried to convince herself of this as much as the others.

She'd been speaking of Dominicus the Merciless. And his brother was rumored to be equally as malevolent. Her widened gaze stared through the window into the dark stormy night.

Simone was unable to calm herself. "I can't take the pressure!" she cried. "If he dies, we would… we would…" Her eyes were stretched to the limit and looked as if they would exit their sockets. "If he dies, I will run for my life!" she exclaimed. But then she thought more of it. "No! Even if we ran—and per chance made it out of his terrible kingdom—our own queen would track us down! Kill us! And the prince! Oh, the dark

Prince! He'll catch us! Maim us! A torturous death! He'll behead us himself! Oh no! Let me out of here!" Having lost herself in hysterics, she was shaking the carriage trying to get to the door.

Cosette grabbed her and held her and attempted to settle her down to no avail. Finally, Ava slapped her. "Get hold of yourself," she said firmly.

Simone became silent, but was otherwise unaffected. With Cosette still holding her arms, she stared blankly into nothingness and made one last statement. "If he dies, I shall jump from the highest cliff."

Cosette looked at Ava with raised eyebrows, and Ava threw her hands in the air, having given up.

Soon, the coachmen hollered whoa to the horses and the carriage came to a stop. The ladies swallowed hard and peered through the window. They had arrived at their destination.

# Chapter Seven

The ladies were led to their quarters. They remained silent the entire time, nonchalantly taking in the ominous, unlit scenery. There were no 'cobwebs' as far as they could see, or 'servants with black eyes', although they did hear what sounded like a scream, but the sound soon faded.

The place had a murky, very dark air about it—a gloom, a shadow of sorts that seemed to blanket the entire castle. They were taken down a long corridor that appeared to have no doors at all until the end where they took several stairs up to a private floor split into three rooms. Wall sconces were already lit in preparation for the three servants. Each room had an old mahogany four poster bed; and bath towels, water, and bedclothes were already there.

They each took to their own rooms and unpacked. Ava was ready to check on the great king at once. She felt they shouldn't waste a single moment not knowing his true condition. She quickly pulled loose the cord of her cloak and called to the other ladies.

Her room was at the immediate entrance of that private floor. She slid back her hood and turned around to see the prince standing in the doorway.

"Alucio–" she said, but corrected herself because of the circumstances. "Prince Alucio, Your Royal Highness," she said and curtsied to him immediately.

He wore no fancy attire, no jacket, no regalia; merely black pants and a white tunic that hung loosely as if he'd worn it for days. His hair hung about his face and he looked tired, saddened, worn out by all of this.

"My beautiful Ava, come to me," he said.

She threw off the cape and immediately obliged. He held her tightly in his arms. She could tell that he was grieving for his brother, but she would not ask him.

The other women entered the room, ready to be escorted to the king.

"Come," said Alucio, and he motioned for them to follow. "We must go now. I will show you what they've done to my brother."

Neither woman spoke, but followed the prince of Dread in silence as they ambled the length of the dark castle. Their footsteps echoed in the halls; the cold chill of death tickled their exposed skin.

Simone jumped suddenly at the loud toll of what must be a large bell somewhere in the castle. It alerted the time of three o'clock. She slapped her hand to her chest and tried to silence her shallow breaths. Alucio and the others turned to look at her as they continued on. She lowered her eyes and tightened her lips.

When they entered a large corridor lit by torches, the prince bade them to wait a moment. Using a key, he entered a room through two very large wooden doors and closed the doors behind him. This was obviously the king's private chambers.

As they waited, Ava fiddled with her fingers, quietly thinking about the injured king. He was so virile and strong. It was difficult to imagine him hurt in any way. Cosette pondered a similar thought, hoping he would soon heal. But Simone again lost focus of the matter at hand and stared deep into the darkness from whence they'd come, wondering what evil was lurking about.

"Simone, what's the matter this time?" asked Cosette.

Simone returned to her senses. "It's nothing," she said.

Suddenly the double doors opened and two male servants and a maid left swiftly. The prince appeared and waved the three women inside. What they saw, none of them could have imagined.

The women were astonished and had to catch their breaths. Although they had attempted to prepare themselves, the sight of the most feared ruler in the land lying helpless and weak at their mercy was overwhelming… and ultimately heartbreaking.

"May we approach him, Your Highness?"
Ava asked the prince.

He motioned them to do so. They reached
the ebony, canopied bed and their eyes washed
over him with anguish and concern as he slept.

"May I touch him?" Ava asked.

"Yes," Alucio answered.

She gently took the hand of the great king.
He was in a deep sleep—one he would not easily
wake from. His eyes were still, his lips unmoving,
and his chest rose and fell with great effort as he
breathed. The king's skin was pale, but warm.
Hints of his age spoke from the small but
distinctive lines about his eyes. The subtle strands
of silver in his hair now spoke of the severity of
his life, as did the lack of lines concerning his
mouth. The woman had never looked at him this
closely before; never had the chance or
permission.

Traces of the blood that had soaked his hair
remained. And blood-drenched bandages adorned
his waist and right shoulder.

Cosette and Simone stood at the foot of the
bed. Sorrow pained them. Ava turned to the

heartbroken but ever-powerful prince. "Your Highness—" she started.

"You may call me Alucio, Ava," he said with great sincerity.

She lowered her head slightly and looked to the king as if for permission. Alucio saw this and answered her thoughts, "Even in the presence of the king," he said.

She would do as he wished. "I am glad to be of service, Alucio, but I am compelled to ask, why were we called?"

Alucio inhaled deeply. "Ava, Simone, Cosette," said Alucio. "I am afraid there is someone in our castle who is an ally to Prince Ethan, an emissary. Until we find out who that is, we must be extremely cautious as to whom we give our trust."

The women were surprised to hear such news.

"My brother was knocked from his steed with a sword. A sword through his right shoulder." He swallowed with great difficulty. "He was then taken to rather badly in the gut by another horse."

Their mouths fell open at the utter notion, and each instinctively touched their own waists.

"Then there isn't much time," cautioned Ava, as she rolled up her sleeves. "We must make sure he can even swallow, for he must drink. Water will be vital to his healing. But first, we will carefully change his bandages. Why are they so bloody? When were they last changed? Alucio, where may I clean my hands?"

Alucio pointed behind her where she found two large freshly-filled basins of water. There were also bowls with which to fill with the water and clean bandages and rags. The servants wouldn't delay. They quickly began their duties.

# Chapter Eight

Cosette prepared all of the king's meals and
served them to his bedchamber whether or not he
was awake or able to eat. The house servants were
told that the king had awoken and was not to be
disturbed. Other than the prince, no one but Ava,
Simone, and Cosette was to know his true
condition.

Simone was charged with keeping the king's
chambers immaculate at all times, and with
replacing the down in his pillows each day. She
would also warm water for his bathing and
provide clean wash towels. Ava tended carefully

to the king's wounds and also kept record of his progress. The prince kept watch over the king while the others slept.

Over the next few days, the king had begun to stir, but had not yet awoken completely. To the servants' relief, and when timed correctly, they were able to get him to swallow small amounts of water when he was most restless, but he had not yet begun to move his arms or open his eyes. They felt the king was in a state where he thought he was dreaming, but was not yet conscious.

Cosette had begun making him stocks that could be swallowed in place of water on occasion. This would help to keep him alive. They were hopeful of this progress, but still, he was not awake. The danger had not yet passed.

Apart from their duties, the three servants were asked to feel at home, and to never mind the noises in the nighttime hours. The prince forbade them to leave the castle during this wretched war, but gave them permission to roam the inside as they pleased.

One night, tired from a long day caring for the king, the women laid on Simone's bed in the dark. They gazed at the moonlit ceiling conversing about recent events.

"King Dominicus... it's just terrible," said Cosette.

"Yes, it is. But he is strong," said Ava. "He will pull through."

"I truly hope so, said Cosette. "I feel he is healing, but without enough food and water... I cannot bear the thought. He is still so frail. And Alucio—I fear Prince Ethan should watch his head."

Simone touched her own throat and cringed at the thought of a beheading, while the other two continued to converse.

"Alucio! Did you see him throw that man out of his way and storm into the library?" asked Cosette.

"Yes," said Simone. "It was terrifying."

"I was with the king, remember?" said Ava. "Tell me, why he was angry?"

"He'd just received a note," said Cosette.

"And he nearly choked the life out of the messenger!" Simone exclaimed.

"And—he told the messenger that he would be delivering a message of his own to Ethan!" said Cosette.

"I wonder what he meant by that," said Ava.

"Whatever he meant, it has me uneasy to say the least," said Cosette.

Simone spoke quietly. "Do you know what has me nervous?"

"What?" the others asked.

"The fact that Alucio told us to 'never mind' the noises in the nighttime hours!" Her eyes were large. "What did that mean?"

Cosette chortled. "It was nothing, I'm sure."

"Nothing?" Simone rasped. "How can you remain so blasé about all of this? This kingdom is peculiar, solemn—it is a terrifying place to be! I think Hell is right beneath this floor. I felt it. The floor really is warm."

"Simone, you are killing us!" said Cosette. "Your mind leaves a little more each day."

"Then touch the floor," she implored them, "Touch it!"

After rolling their eyes, Cosette and Ava decided to humor Simone by touching the floor. They climbed off the bed and got on their hands and knees. Cosette started to laugh, "Aha! Oh wait, it is warm."

"What did I tell you?" Simone huffed. "I tell you this place has an ominous air about it. Something wicked lurks." She watched as Ava and Cosette seemed to see something under the bed.

"That is odd," said Ava, as the two leaned closer to see what it was.

Simone leaned over the bed to see. "Boo!" said Ava and Cosette in unison.

Simone screamed and the others fell over in laughter. "Thank you, Simone," said Ava. "We needed a brief moment of joy."

"But what if they heard me scream, you foolish girls," warned Simone.

"Screams are normal around here. Remember, Simone?" said Cosette impishly.

"Forget the both of you!" Simone yelled before hiding under the covers.

Later, Ava and Cosette had gone to sleep. They were concerned for the king and anxious to finish their four hours of sleep so they could return to their duties. Simone lay awake, watching the shadows move along the walls. They seemed to come from nowhere. As she clenched her blankets to her chin in a vice-like grip, she heard a scream from somewhere below. "Someone being tortured," she thought. Then she heard a creaking sound. It had come from across the room. When her eyes acclimated to the moonlight, she could just make out that a secret door was opening in the wall across from her bed. Her heart began to pound as she watched only by the light of the moon. She couldn't move. Once it was completely open, she heard footsteps nearing her bed. She quickly closed her eyes. "I'm home, I'm home, I'm home," she told herself.

Even in the ominous castle, a dark and unfamiliar place, Cosette laid in bed soundly, a wicked grin upon her lips. She was dreaming of how they'd frightened Simone. Ava smiled in her sleep as well. She too had subconsciously recalled the prank, but suddenly her dreams turned to the king and to his brother, a man she'd quickly come to care for. Ava felt for the prince in the closest possible way. And his pain distressed her heart tremendously. She began to toss and turn in her sleep.

Simone, awake and trembling, finally managed to open her eyes. A figure was nearing her bed. "Please go away," she insisted. "I have a weapon."

Suddenly, a man covered her mouth. She tried to scream but it was muffled. He slid his hand under the sheet and along her smooth leg. She stretched her arm and grabbed hold of the candle holder and cracked it over his head.

"Ow!" he yelled.

"Erec?" said Simone as he toppled over.

Simone lit a candle and saw him lying on the floor groaning and holding his head.

"Why did you cover my mouth?" she scolded.

"I knew you'd scream," said Erec. "But I didn't think you'd hit me. That hurt."

"That's exactly what you deserve for scaring me," she said. "I was enjoying a peaceful night's sleep until you barged in here like some ruffian."

She helped him onto the bed then peeked into the other rooms to see if the others had awoken. Seeing they had not, she returned to him, seductively. "Now—where does it hurt?" she asked.

"Right here," he said, pulling her in for a kiss.

# Chapter Nine

As the battle waged over the next few days, Ava, Cosette, and Simone made certain King Dominicus was given the best care and attention possible. He wanted for nothing. He'd begun to open his eyes and to speak softly, albeit with some difficulty; and he even smiled and winked at his three new servants. He could only stay awake for short intervals, but he was beginning to heal, and they were overjoyed at his progress.

But the king's brother was becoming increasingly stressed. Ava wished she could help, but she didn't think that would be possible—until one afternoon…

After the king fell to sleep, Ava and Simone locked the door behind them and went to meet with Cosette in the kitchen. They took a walk through the courtyard until they came upon a garden with a huge stone fountain. In the center of the fountain stood three maiden statues encircling a male figure. One bathed him, another filled his mouth with the water that poured from her pitcher and the third kneeled at his feet. Her breasts were exposed as if to pleasure his eyes, and there was a dagger tucked into her belt.

The women sat and talked about the king, Prince Alucio, and the terrible Ethan.

"When will this be over?" Simone wondered aloud.

The others shook their heads.

"I don't know, Simone," said Ava. "It is just terrible. I heard that another four knights are returning injured. Alucio is very near the edge. I wish there was something more we could do."

"We all do, Ava. But what?" said Cosette, remorsefully. "I've been snooping around and listening in on conversations, trying to discover the traitor. But I haven't uncovered a thing."

"And I've been trying to help too," said Simone. "I've sneaked into bedrooms, gone through drawers and closets, and followed people around to see what they are up to. You simply can't trust anyone anymore."

"I know," said Cosette. "It's a shame really."

Just then, a young maid came running toward the three servants. She was waving one hand in the air and holding her dress out of the way with the other.

"Ladies, please!" she shouted, half out of breath.

"Oh, no! Is it the king?" asked Ava.

"No, it is not His Majesty!" cried the girl. "It's Sir Lazander. It's terrible!"

The women gasped. "Is he alive?" she asked.

"Yes, he is hurt, but not badly," said the girl. "He returned to report to His Royal Highness the prince, but he…" The maid could hardly breathe for speaking too quickly.

Ava's eyes grew large. She grabbed the woman by the shoulders. "What about the prince?"

This frightened the maid and she swallowed hard and continued. "His Highness left this morning to catch up to Lazander and Erec, to lead the army himself. But Sir Lazander says no one has seen the prince at all!"

Ava's heart stopped.

"Madams, there has been no word of the prince since he left this morning, and now 'tis nearly dusk."

Cosette and Simone grabbed onto Ava as she appeared faint.

"Ethan is winning this," said Simone. "What will we do?"

Her eyes wet with worry, the maid hurried back to her duties.

"We have to do something," said Cosette.

Ava looked up and eyed the fountain, however this time she stared a little more closely. Her mind became very clear.

"What is it, Ava?" asked the others.

"The fountain," she replied. "It's three women taking care of the man. Do you see what it represents?" she asked. "Think it through. Women always have the advantage. Men are putty in our hands! We are their weakness! Look closely—one woman is quenching his thirst, one woman bathes him, and the other woman seduces him—but it's a distraction. There is a dagger tucked into her belt—for use if necessary."

Cosette began to understand, but Simone was lost. "You lost me at 'thirst'," she said.

Ava turned to Simone with a sinister grin. "My friend, we will stop Ethan ourselves. We shall use our womanly charms to get close—and then strike with our daggers."

Cosette's mouth curved into a sated grin.

Simone remained blank. "Where are we going to get daggers?"

"We'll explain on the way," said Cosette.

# Chapter Ten

Ava, Simone, and Cosette tended to King Dominicus with their usual diligence and care. As night began to fall, no word of the prince had yet been heard. The servants bided their time, waiting for their chance to slip away. They didn't wish to leave the king, but he was nearly healed and most of his time was spent resting peacefully. They took it upon themselves to appoint an elderly woman by the name of Dorothea to keep an eye on him. Alucio had shown trust in her and she had been with them for many years. She would arrive soon.

The stroke of midnight donned from the bell tower above the castle. A frightening sound it made, appropriate for the kingdom of Dread. It gave Simone shivers each time it rang, but this time, it alerted them it was time to go.

Ava slipped into the room of the injured king while her counterparts waited quietly in the dark hallway. She crept over to the desk table, and, using His Majesty's quill and ink, began to script a note for him.

*Your Grand Magnificence, King Dominicus,*

*We write to inform you of our necessary absence. In this time of dire straits, we feel it is our duty to take the matter of the battle into our own hands. We—*

Ava was suddenly interrupted when she noticed Cosette looking over her shoulder. "You're going to say it that way?" she queried.

"Cosette! Shh! You'll wake the king!" she warned in a stern whisper. "And will you mind your own business? You're supposed to be waiting in the hall!"

"Well, you were taking an awfully long time," said Cosette. "And now I come in and see you writing this nonsense."

"Well, excuse me, Miss Chaucer," Ava huffed. "What would you like to say in the note?"

Cosette sucked in her lips and thought hard for a moment. Then she snatched the quill from her friend and dipped it into the ink. Ava simply stared at her now empty fingertips.

"Ah, yes, how about this?" asked Cosette.

She'd scratched out Ava's last line and wrote under it:

*...we feel it is our duty to sneak behind enemy lines and overthrow the battle so that—*

"Give me that quill!" Ava spat, abruptly taking back the feathered writing tool. "Don't be ridiculous, 'overthrow the battle'. Really." She immediately scratched out Cosette's last line.

Cosette stood straighter. Her eyes like daggers. "What do you mean 'ridiculous'? Yours was ridiculous!"

"Shh!" warned Ava. "A million times, keep it down! You'll wake the king!"

The women tried desperately to keep quiet, they couldn't risk being heard and caught.

"Well, let's say, 'conquer' then," said Cosette.

"Actually, that's not so bad," whispered Ava. "But what about 'surmount'?"

"No, no—now it's getting silly," said Cosette. "How about 'overcome'? 'Ey? That's good, no? Uh-huh, that's definitely it."

Cosette nodded her head proudly, but Ava just stared at her blankly. "Overcome? Now that is just idiotic."

Cosette gasped. "How dare you call my—"

Just then, Simone slipped from behind them and spoke in a normal indoor voice. "How about 'defeat'?"

Cosette and Ava jumped with fright and Ava dropped the quill.

"Simone!" they whispered loudly.

"What are you doing in here?" said Ava. "The king! The king! You'll wake him!"

"You were taking too long so I came to see what was—"

The king began to stir in his blankets. Ava and Cosette froze in place and stared at him, their breathing ceased.

Simone began to panic. "Oh no," she said aloud. "He's waking—"

But Simone couldn't finish her statement because Cosette quickly covered her mouth with her hand and placed a letter-opener to her throat.

Simone didn't breathe, but the others didn't either. They waited, and when he stopped moving, all of them let out a huge sigh of relief.

"Thank the spirits!" said Ava. "Now, where is that quill? Honestly!"

She found the quill and threw the old note in the fireplace. On a fresh piece of parchment, she wrote:

*Your Supreme Magnificence,*

*We are leaving, against Prince Alucio's direct orders, but we feel compelled to do something about this unending battle. Whether or not we return, please forgive us.*

*Your loyal and humble servants,*

*Ava, Cosette, and Simone*

Cosette's hand remained over Simone's mouth as they crept ever-so-slowly out of the king's chambers and into the hall. Dorothea had arrived. She looked at the hand over Simone's mouth with some confusion. Cosette simply smiled at her as Ava ushered the woman inside. She then released an angry Simone.

Oblivious, Cosette turned to Ava with a stern look in her eyes. "You just had to put your name first on the note, didn't you?"

The other women just shook their heads and picked up their totes. Ava gestured the way, and they sneaked out of the castle.

## Chapter Eleven

The women took off into the cold night. They were very surprised at how easily they had been able to escape the kingdom unseen. "I am beginning to like sneaking around. It's exciting," said Simone, as they crept across the grassy fields.

As they reached the edge of the kingdom, they began to smell the aroma of meat being cooked over a fire.

"Stop," Cosette whispered, extending her arms to keep the others from going. "I think we just found Ethan's camp."

They saw the smoke rising about fifty yards to the northwest. They saw no soldiers and no battle nearby.

Ava whispered, "I just can't believe we got this close and have seen no guards."

"Let us not speak so soon," suggested Cosette. "We should take this time to make doubly sure we have our stories straight. Remember, we have escaped the control of our abusive master, Cornelius, and have been traveling on foot for six moons. Now we've run out of money and have no place to go."

"That's right," says Ava.

"Got it," said Simone. "And each of us was sold to him by our parents when we were children. And if we become separated after we're captured, we will still move forward with the plan."

"All right," said Cosette. "We do this for the king, for the people, and for Prince Alucio. We must keep our composure at any cost—no matter what we see or hear."

When all were in agreement, they headed for the camp. They walked about twenty yards and were swiftly captured.

To be captured was precisely what the women wanted. They knew it would be their only means of getting inside enemy lines and close to Prince Ethan of Aldren. But they had no idea just how quickly they would get to meet the dastardly prince.

"Get in there, peasants!" barked one of the hefty guards as he muscled Cosette into a large tent. Two other guards forced the Ava and Simone inside as well. The ladies found themselves on their knees on the dirt floor before the prince himself.

He was a handsome man. He was tall, with short dark hair, a clean goatee and sharp green eyes. Ava tried to hold back an evil glare as she looked at this smug man. He was so sure of himself. She thought of King Dominicus and of Prince Alucio. She would find Alucio and kill this man. As her eyes began to narrow, Cosette threw her a cautionary stare and Ava quickly let her eyes fall back to the ground unnoticed.

"What have we here?" said Ethan to his guards.

"We found them lurking in the woods, Your Highness," said a guard. "But they could be infiltrators."

"Infiltrators?" said Ethan. He leaned down to Simone and lifted her by the hand gently. "Three beauties like these could not be spies—could you milady?"

"No sir… I mean… No, Your Highness," said Simone, smelling the robust stench of liquor on his breath.

"I didn't think so," he said.

He took a flask from his hip and downed a bit more of his drink. It was very strong, and even Cosette, from two yards away, recognized the scent to be that of a very fine whiskey.

Ethan stroked Simone's cheek and grinned seductively. "Are you three ladies alone?"

"Yes," they answered.

"All alone in these dark woods you say?"

"Yes," said Simone.

"You are very clean for peasants," said Ethan with suspicion in his eyes. He motioned Cosette and Ava to stand beside their friend.

"We've bathed recently," said Ava.

Ethan went to Ava, who had spoken out of turn, and gazed over her carefully. "Where did you bathe?" he asked. His voice was soft and full of warning. He was trying to catch them in a lie and they were fully aware.

Cosette and Simone became even more nervous. They had not been prepared for this particular question.

Ava did not stall for a moment. "We bathed in the river Nera," she said convincingly.

To their tremendous relief, Ethan believed her. "I should have liked to have been there to watch," he said brazenly.

Ava was anxious to change the topic of conversation. "If I may speak openly, Your Highness," she said.

Ethan was pleased with her gentility and nodded.

"You see," she continued, "We were forced to leave our home, and have run out of money. I'm afraid we've no place to—"

He waved his hand in the air to halt her speech. "Say no more," he said. "You will stay with me."

"But, Your Highness—" Ava pretended to protest.

"No, it is settled," he said. "I am ruler of this land, and you will be of special service to me. I cannot turn away such lovely creatures as you." He took Cosette by the neck in a sensual manner, "It would be coldhearted of me," he whispered in her ear.

She was repulsed, but alas, could do nothing. She smiled coyly as if his manner pleased her.

He then licked the side of her face. She held back her fury. Ava and Simone were very calm.

Suddenly Ethan yelled, "Guards! I want you to take these women by carriage to my castle, and see to it that they are prepared for me when I arrive. I'll be there shortly."

Ethan guzzled his drink once more. "And see to it that a fine malt whiskey is waiting by my bedside."

"As you wish, Your Majesty," someone said.

Bedside? Ava thought to herself. She'd expected as much, but not so soon. She secretly ground her teeth.

Ethan walked up to Ava and pulled at the lace of her top. He inhaled her sent as if he were drinking her in, then he sent the women away with the guards.

The women were relieved to be leaving his presence for a time, and glad that their plan was working so well. He liked them. That was the first step. They were doing a tremendous job remaining calm, until he made one last comment on their way out.

"Ladies, soon this war will be over," he said. "And I will have taken the palace of Dread. The brothers will be gone and I will reign supreme. You'll want me as your friend. Remember that."

They just smiled and turned to leave. They wanted nothing more than to stab him to death right then and there. But however difficult it might be, they would bide their time.

## Chapter Twelve

They traveled some distance to Ethan's castle. The road was rough. Two guards accompanied the women inside the carriage and stared at them quite imposingly. The three ladies were hesitant to question why they stared, instead they held their tongues. They chose not to uncover what the traitorous oafs could possibly be thinking. Alas, however, one of the men spoke. "Don't sass him," was all he mustered. He stared at Cosette as he said this, and she lifted her eyes to meet his.

"Pardon?" she said.

"Beware your tongue with Ethan," said the guard.

The women weren't certain of it, but the guard sounded as if he was trying to help by giving them advice.

"If you mind your tongue, he will treat you like a queen. But if he thinks you question his authority–"

The other guard interrupted by kicking at his boot. The guard then clammed up. The women returned their eyes to their laps and secretly took note of this brush with kindness. They knew it was unlikely to happen again.

Upon arrival, the women were aghast at the look of the place. The castle was rather modest in comparison to the Palace of Dread. It was taller than it was long, and weathered, with many spalling stones. On one side was a tower with one lighted window at the top.

"Eyes ahead," boomed the officious voice of one of the guards.

As they were led inside, just as they were turning away from the tower, someone appeared at its lone window. The guards didn't seem to notice and the women said nothing.

The women were not led through the main doors, but through a small door in the back. They saw no caretakers and no servants the entire journey to the bedroom. They were informed that it was also Prince Ethan's room. They cringed at the notion and further realized what they had gotten themselves into.

It was a large room, yet much smaller than that of the king. And it was kempt, but dusty and the floor was not swept. The women placed their bags on a tattered divan and turned in time to see the guards take leave. The one who'd spoken to them briefly in the carriage was the last to exit.

Cosette boldly took his arm. "What is your name?"

He was quite surprised by her action. "John," he replied.

He turned to leave and then looked back hesitantly. Once he was certain that the other guard had gone, he whispered, "He likes to drink." His eyes fell onto the liquor chest and the ladies immediately knew what he meant. John then closed the door and left.

They seemed to have one ally in the castle of Aldren, but they would be wary still.

Dorothea was nervous. She cared deeply for her king, and was fiercely loyal. She was an elderly lady, and took no gruff from anybody. But the mood about the kingdom was an anxious one. Someone in Dread Kingdom was an ally to Prince Ethan and she would trust no one to get near the king. She was on edge. The unusual quiet in the castle unnerved her, and she kept her ears perked up for the slightest sound. She kept the door to His Majesty's chambers both locked and barricaded. His chambers were stocked for times such as these. They wouldn't have to leave it for several days. She hoped that was enough time.

Dorothea approached the sleeping king and dabbed his forehead with a cool rag. He went through fluctuating periods of fever and this always seemed to help.

Suddenly, she heard the faintest sound of footsteps nearing the door. Someone was treading very lightly.

Her eyes became fixed on the knob of the door. It began to turn slowly until the turner found it locked. No one knocked or uttered a word.

It then sounded as if the person had gone. Dorothea sighed with relief, but then someone did speak. As if altering his voice, a man asked, "Dorothea? Are you there?"

She was hesitant at first. What person in this kingdom would turn the king's door knob without announcing himself first? No one would. She didn't trust this man, but chose not to rouse suspicion. "Yes, I am here. Who is calling?"

The man did not respond to her question, but instead replied, "I am merely inquiring about the king. Is he much better?"

"Oh yes," said Dorothea. "He was just up a while ago enjoying a tankard of mead," she lied.

The man was silent and then left. Dorothea knew he'd been up to something.

At Ethan's castle, Ava, Cosette, and Simone changed clothes and prepared for the evil prince. When he arrived, he immediately took to his bedchamber where the ladies were anxiously waiting.

Cosette greeted him at the door. "Why, Your Highness, we thought you'd never arrive," she said seductively while tracing his bristly jawline with her fingertips.

The other two ladies were sprawled upon the bed trying to look their most alluring. Ethan was pleasantly surprised. "Well, well, well," he said. "How nice. Most women are diffident when they arrive in my bedchamber. You three seem to know what you want. It's refreshing to say the least."

"Oh yes," Cosette whispered. "We know exactly what we want, and mean to get it." She pulled him by the hand to the bed.

Ava and Simone made him sit while Cosette poured him a drink. He gulped the dark fluid and slammed the cup down. The woman began to remove his jacket and shirt. When they reached his belt and scabbard, he quickly covered the hilt of the sword with this hand and looked suspiciously at the women. They halted. Then he smiled and removed the sword belt himself.

While Ava and Simone massaged his bare back and shoulders, Cosette kept refilling his drink and urging him to down it in droves. He became more inebriated with each passing moment—just what the women wanted. His awareness was waning. While Cosette began to untie her top, his eyes were fixed upon her bosom, awaiting the view. As this transpired, Ava slipped a dagger from beneath the pillows and raised it high in the air. Ethan's back was to her as she prepared to end his life...

But someone banged at the door. "Your Highness! Urgent news!" a voice boomed.

Cosette scoffed and retied her laces, and Ava quickly hid the dagger as Ethan ambled to the door and opened it. "It had better be important!" Ethan blasted.

The burly guard insisted that it was. "Your Highness, I have received word that King Dominicus has risen. Apparently, he has been up and drinking mead."

The blood drained from Ethan's face. The ladies didn't know what to make of this news. How could this man know such a thing? Prince Alucio was right. There was a spy in Dread Kingdom, and what's worse, they were inside the castle.

Ethan grabbed his shirt and sword belt and stormed out of the room.

"Damn!" shouted Cosette. "We almost had him!"

Ava was also quite angry. "We had him in our clutches," she growled.

Cosette agreed. "I am ready to storm the entire castle until we find him then ambush him right where he stands."

Simone had an idea of her own. "I'll bet he's left the castle. He is probably at his camp."

Cosette and Ava gazed at Simone with astonishment. Her words had sparked the same idea in both of them. She was probably right. All of his men seemed to be at the camp, so where else would he have gone to handle such business?

Cosette eased her way to the door to give a listen. Once certain no one was outside the door and that the hall was quiet, she inched back to the women and spoke in a low, plotting whisper. "What say we sneak around the castle a bit and see what else we can learn about this Ethan fellow?"

Ava was in full agreement. "And find the location of the dungeon," she said. "Maybe they have Prince Alucio locked away." She nearly choked on those words.

The ladies looked at each other with hopeful eyes, but knew the chances were slim. Simone, however, also pondered what the dark prince would do if he discovered they had left his brother, the king. She shuttered to think, but they were in far too deep to turn back now.

They unlocked the door and crept out into the dim corridor. There seemed to be no sounds from anywhere. It gave them an eerie feeling—more so even than the dark castle of Dread. The silence was deafening. It was such a quiet that Simone was almost certain she was being watched. But they saw no one.

The ladies sneaked cagily through the castle. It wasn't enormous, but wasn't so small that they could scour its entirety before Prince Ethan returned. They knew they should make their rounds swiftly, so they went only to the main rooms of the castle. They found each corner of the castle to be vacant. Somehow, they seemed to be alone in the entire place.

The women made their way back to the kitchen, which was the closest room to the corridor to Ethan's room. Simone and Cosette boldly sat at the round wooden table and attempted to slice some stale bread.

"Would he really have left us alone?" Simone asked.

Ava peered cautiously through the back door. She could see the lights from Ethan's camp in the distance. "Yes," she answered. "By the looks of this place, Ethan's army isn't very large. Every subject of Aldren is probably out there in the field."

Suddenly Ava's eyes climbed the tower to the lonely lighted window. "I am curious though... why haven't we found any stairs that descend to a dungeon? And why not a staircase leading up to that tower?"

"That's right!" said Cosette. She joined Ava at the door. "The tower is connected. Do you see? There must be an entrance, but where could it be?"

Simone joined the ladies and suddenly a silhouette appeared at the tower's window. The women were frozen still. As their eyes remained on the figure, it began to move. It appeared to be a woman. Then, all at once, the figure moved out of sight.

The women stammered back inside and closed the door.

"We must get to the top of that tower. Maybe that woman can help us!" Cosette insisted.

"You're right," said Ava. "And I think I know the way," she smirked. She'd just realized the tower was the only part of the castle east and above Ethan's chambers. The pathway was certainly through his room. "Follow me. We must get back to the bedroom."

"That's a good idea," a low voice rumbled form behind them.

They turned quickly and were relieved to see John standing before them. "John! It's you! Thank goodness. Are you alone?"

"Yes," he whispered. "But you must hurry, Ethan is close behind. Return to his room immediately." He ushered them into the corridor.

"But John," Cosette besieged, "There is a woman in the tower—"

John's eyes became large. "You must stay away from there. Never you mind such things. Now go! He nears!"

Cosette turned reluctantly, and Ava and Simone pulled her down the hall by the arm. They nearly tripped over their skirts and stumbled into the room.

Prince Ethan and a guard arrived by the kitchen door where the women had just been standing. They hadn't seen the women, but did arrive in time to see John turn around. Ethan had suspicion in his eyes. "Midnight snack, Sir John?"

John immediately saw the broken bread on the table and quickly covered. "Yes," he lied, "I was famished, haven't eaten since yesterday's supper."

Ethan slapped the man's shoulder. "You shouldn't be so mindless of your appetite, man. During these arduous hours my men need to keep their strength."

"Yes, of course, Your Highness."

Both men chuckled and Ethan left for his chambers.

## Chapter Thirteen

When Ethan arrived in his chambers, he found the women to be waiting patiently. Little did he know, they'd been lying in wait. He slowly closed and latched his door and grinned smugly at the enticing ladies.

Cosette returned to his side to pick up where they'd left off, but this time the women had other plans. They would not kill him yet, for they had other business in the castle. They wanted to question the woman in the tower. If they waited until the prince was dead, they would have no time, as they would have to immediately run for the border of Dread Kingdom. Instead they would have to delay his murder until afterward.

In the meantime, the sinister prince had a revoltingly lustful gleam in his eye. They would have to play along. They hoped they could get him to pass out from drunkenness before it went too far.

Simone poured him a fresh drink. With one hand, he thanked her bosom, and with the other he raised the mug and downed the fluid with one forceful chug. He then turned to Cosette and pushed her to the bed. "Why don't you show me what you started to earlier?" He ordered with a grin.

She swallowed hard. Somehow, he wasn't drunk enough yet, and she didn't want to strip completely. But he didn't appear to be very patient. Cosette slowly began to unlace her dress. Ava tried to help by distracting him. She crawled across the bed and pulled him closer to her by his belt buckle. He stumbled forward happily and Simone handed him another full mug of whiskey. He drank it down and turned his now blurry gaze back to Cosette. "I thought I told you to undress," he growled. Cosette and Simone both tensed at his dark tone.

Ava knew she had to do something fast. She began to unbuckle his belt with her teeth. This got his complete attention. He seemed to forget about the other two women and was consumed by the delightful forwardness of this exotic beauty. He unfastened the roll of her hair and the dark tresses fell over her shoulders. She was disgusted by this man but would do whatever it took to protect her friends and to avenge the wrongs done to Alucio and Dominicus.

His sword belt dropped. Using her teeth, she unlaced the cord of his breeches. Simone filled his drink once more. They hoped he wasn't too distracted to drink it.

His head began to slouch and rock as he stared at Ava and tried to focus. He took a drink and began to stumble, but Simone braced him. Ava stood and moved him to the bed. She pressed into his chest with just a little force to get him to the straw-filled mattress. Cosette moved out of the way. As he lied back onto his pillows, Ethan stared at Ava as she glared into his eyes. He thought he saw malice in her for a moment, but was too inebriated to ponder it. Instead, his mind returned to his lust-filled thoughts.

Simone and Ava slipped his pants off, much to his enjoyment. Then he drank some more. Ava then crawled up his repulsive body with feigned desire and kissed his chest. He breathed deeply. Inside she was nauseous, but the job had to be done. She was stalling him with foreplay. She kissed his navel and then just below the navel. When she got too low, she moved her lips to his hip and he reached up and grabbed her hair. He moved her head to a better place and just as the three women gulped with dread, his hand dropped cold. He was passed out.

They'd never breathed such sighs of relief.

The women helped Ava off of the bed quietly and the three held each other for a moment. Cosette stared deeply into her friend's eyes revealing her appreciation. Ava answered the gesture. "We knew what we were getting into by coming here."

"I know," said Cosette. "But thank you anyway."

"You would have done the same for me," replied Ava.

"Without hesitation," Cosette smiled. "Now let's find the secret passage and get to that tower. He'll be out for hours."

The women refastened their clothing and Ava tied up her hair. Simone then enlightened them with some terrific news. "I found it," she said with a cheerful grin.

In the corner across from Ethan's bed Simone stood by a now open false wall. The passage was dark and a cold draft poured from it. The three women hurriedly slipped into the dark opening and closed the wall behind them.

"You're a genius, Simone!" Cosette whispered loudly.

Simone half-grinned. "Praise me later, when we're sure we can get back in!"

All the women gasped at that thought of being trapped, but there was nothing they could do about it now. They had to press on.

They found that the passageway led to many rooms. They didn't seem to be accessible, but had secret holes for spying. It was perfect for a sinister prince who wanted to spy on other possible traitors—or anyone else.

Soon, they began to ascend a narrow staircase. "This must be the way!" whispered Ava.

The stairs seemed to go on forever, but alas, they arrived at the top. The women took turns peeping through the secret crevice. At first, they saw no one, but then the sound of sobbing came from the right. Cosette strained to see the woman and then she came into view. She was a beautiful redhead dressed like a queen. Ava and Simone had a look. They were flabbergasted. She wasn't what they were expecting. Why would such a woman be locked away like this?

Cosette could wait no longer to find out. She suddenly burst open the door. The regal-looking woman cowered in the corner without looking to see who it was. "No!" the woman cried. "Not tonight. Please leave!"

"Pardon?" Cosette asked, her friends appearing at her sides.

The woman was shocked. She looked at the three women and staggered to her full height. "Where... where is Ethan?" she asked.

"He sleeps in his bed," Simone replied.

The lady looked puzzled. "How did you get in here? Who are you?"

Cosette neared her. "We are new to Aldren. We came to stay with Ethan just tonight."

"Are you friends of Ethan's?"

"No," said Ava. "We are merely servants."

The lady tilted her head slightly with a gleam in her teary eyes. "Shifty servants, I would say."

The three women grinned happily. They knew this mysterious woman was beginning to understand what they were up to—and they had a feeling she didn't mind.

The woman hurried the servants in and slid a rock into the passage door frame so that it wouldn't close. The women realized it only opened from the other side which confirmed their suspicions. No one was meant to leave this room.

"Ethan leaves the rock there so he can come and go," the lady informed them.

"May we ask who you are, milady?" asked Simone.

The woman turned to the window and peered out over the dark land. "My name is Cleona. I am Queen of Aldren. Ethan is my husband."

The servants were overcome with disbelief, and serious concern.

# Chapter Fourteen

Queen Cleona was not very old. She was beautiful and kind, but seemed aged by sadness. The servants were anxious to know how a queen could have come to such circumstances. The moment she said she was queen, they curtsied before her. They didn't lift their heads and she noticed this.

Cleona was taken aback by their graciousness. However, it had been some time since she had been respected as a queen. It seemed like ages since anyone served her, let alone bowed to her. She hardly felt like royalty.

The benevolent queen went to them and asked them to raise their heads. "For the moment, I am no queen. There is no need to bow to me," she said with a smile.

The servants were surprised by this, but were made to feel comfortable by the queen's kindness.

"How long had Ethan been sleeping before you slipped away?" she asked them.

"Only minutes, your majesty," Simone replied.

"You may call me Cleona. Had he been drinking?" she asked.

"Oh, yes," Cosette assured her.

"Then he will be asleep for hours," said Cleona. "Still, you may have to worry about his guards. They will check in on him so you must hurry. First, tell me how you came to this place? What are you doing here?"

The servants explained in detail all that they knew. Cleona relayed her extreme surprise that even Ethan would dare cross the feared king of Dread. She was unnerved, to say the least. If King Dominicus were to unleash his full power, her entire castle and kingdom would cease to exist from that moment forward. She then began to explain how she came to be where she was.

"For three long years, my husband has kept me locked in this tower. He told the kingdom I died of fever and threatened the guards who knew the truth. He emptied the castle of my loyal servants so they would never discover me. What he did with them, I do not know."

"Why don't you come with us now?!" Ava pleaded. "Reclaim your throne! This is the time! And you can stop this war!"

"I cannot," said Cleona. Her eyes drifted to the ground.

Cosette could tell that she was hiding something. "What is it, Cleona? What is his hold on you?"

The servants were listening very intently.

Cleona clasped her locket and began her story. "I didn't mean for it to happen... but I fell in love with another. I never felt so complete in my life as when this man entered it. He felt the same for me. Married or not, queen or not, my heart would not let go. We gave in to our desires. I swear it was true love—it is true love still. Ethan found out about us. He didn't blame the man.

Ethan has always been motivated by one thing, and he assumes all men are. He blamed me for seducing the guard and locked me here indefinitely. Then he took over the throne. He'd wanted it all along. I just made it easier for him."

Cosette was puzzled. "In your absence, is Ethan truly king?"

"No," said Cleona. "He admitted to forging documents declaring him king in the event of my death. And I'm certain he has killed anyone who would question his reign. I am certain, however, that the house of Dread considers him no more than a usurper and a tiresome, unworthy prince. I find some degree of solace in that thought."

Ava felt this was true, as she had only ever heard him referred to as prince, never as king.

"I am sorry to ask," said Cosette, "but, why did Ethan keep you alive?"

"It is a game for Ethan. He can have me whenever he wants," said Cleona. "He makes me submit by threatening the life of my true love."

Simone was nearly in tears.

"Then he is still here? Working for Ethan? You said he was a guard..." Ava recalled.

"I can only hope," the queen sobbed. Her heart was truly breaking. "His name is John."

The servants gasped. "John? We know him! He is the only one who has been kind to us. It must be him!"

The queen wiped her tears and stood quickly. "My John? Is he tall and broad? Does he have red hair the color of mid-autumn and soft lips like down on your skin?" The queen was in a hopeful daze. She'd dreamed he was alive, but was afraid to know the truth.

"Well, we do not know of his lips..." said Cosette, "but he is otherwise as you described. And he has a small scar on his neck."

Simultaneously Cosette and Cleona said "Right here," while touching the same location on their necks.

Cleona's eyes filled with tears of joy. "It is him. It is my John!"

"Then come with us!" Ava pleaded.

Suddenly they heard a loud crashing sound in the corridor. It was of Ethan's door to the passage bursting open. They knew he must have awakened and they began to panic.

Queen Cleona removed the stone from the doorway and closed it. "You must hide quickly!"

"But where?" Simone squealed as she shuffled about the room searching for a drawer to climb into.

Ava and Cosette peered through the window.

"It's too far down," Cleona warned them as she ushered Simone under the bed and tried to force the skirt of her dress under with her foot.

Ava and Cosette agreed and scrambled to find a hiding place. Cleona helped them both into her large but narrow oak wardrobe. Once inside, among her own gowns, she had to tuck their dresses around them wherever she could in order to close the doors. They were certain that if they moved an inch they would either suffocate or the hordes of fabric would burst open the wardrobe doors. They couldn't afford to breathe.

Just as Cleona closed the wardrobe, Prince Ethan flung open the tower door. "You seem quite out of breath my traitorous wife."

Cleona was stammered by his comment and tried to gather herself as she watched him lodge the door open with the stone doorstop.

"You must have been eager to see me," he concluded.

She let out a silent sigh of relief.

Simone watched his boots saunter around the room as she was forced to listen to his hideous voice. She gripped tightly the sides of her dress to keep it from falling into view. Sweat beads formed on her forehead and her heart stilled every time he neared the bed. Eventually he sat there. She gulped hard.

Cleona wanted to rush him along, if possible, but didn't want to rouse his suspicions. "Why did you come here, Ethan?" she asked.

He scoffed and stood to face her. "You know to address me as your king," he reminded.

The three servants were ready to spit nails. His depravity truly knew no bounds. But Queen Cleona was quick with her wit. "You can lock me here for eternity, but I think you know I would sooner call a swine 'king' than you, however redundant," she smarmed.

The servants liked this woman more by the minute. Ethan was furious. He grabbed her by the arm and tossed her to the bed. The wooden slat underneath it pressed into Simone's back. She clenched her teeth to keep from making a sound.

"You insolent witch!" Ethan yelled. Then he slapped the queen with all his might. She didn't cry, but held her face and closed her eyes tightly. She would not let this beast win. He grabbed her by the throat and pulled her closer. "If I didn't have something else to attend to, I would teach you a lesson right now." He then dropped her.

She just glared at him as he climbed off of the bed. He straightened his clothes and gathered his bearings. "You haven't spoken to or heard from anyone—have you?" he asked.

"Of course not. Isn't that why you have me locked up in this tower—to avoid contact with the outside world?" she spat.

He huffed and kicked the stone from the doorway. "Your attitude is wearing thin," he warned. "But it matters naught. By dawn in two days we will have stormed the castle of Dread, and this castle, along with you inside it, will be destroyed." He stormed away, slamming the door.

After several minutes, the four women sighed with relief. He was gone, but likely looking for the three shifty servants.

The four women gathered at the queen's bed. Her face was already beginning to bruise. None of them spoke for several moments. No words were required at that time. Finally, Ava rose from the bed. "How will we get out of here?" she asked.

Cleona stood from the bed and went to the door and opened it. The servants were taken aback. "But how?"

Cleona slid her hand into a knothole on the door frame and slid out a sizable lock of her hair tied with twine. She had slipped it there when Ethan was on his way up. It was to keep the door from fastening so the servants could escape.

"This is my hair, give it to John. Then he will know I live. Tell him my heart beats for him still."

"Then you still mean not to join us?"

"If you can kill Ethan, do. But if you do not succeed, I will still fear for the life of my John. Thus, I must remain here as Ethan demands, or else I put him at risk."

The servants understood. They further understood that Queen Cleona's love for John was steadfast and everlasting. Theirs was a love that people dreamed of. They went to the door.

"Don't go to Ethan's room, he might be there and see you coming."

"Then how will we get out?" asked Cosette.

Cleona smiled. "I know this castle better than Ethan ever will. There is another passage that breaks from this one. You will not see it in the dark. Count eleven- and one-half paces and feel for a notch in the wood above your right shoulder. Slide it and you will open a door to a set of stairs leading to the center of the castle. When the walls become cool, you will be near the water. You will come to a fork where there is a secret door into the dungeon, or you can follow the wall to the water and make your escape."

The women had a lot to digest. They could be moments from escape, but they had come there to get a job done. And although it had been a grave undertaking, they would see it through. Cosette held the tied locks of the queen's hair and took the queen's hand. "Be well, your highness."

And they slipped off into the darkness.

# Chapter Fifteen

The three servants found the second secret passage and made it to the cool, dank fork in their path. They knew this was their chance to escape and attempt to return to Dread Kingdom safely. But they didn't hesitate for a moment, not even Simone. Their task would be done. They found the secret door in the darkness and entered the dungeon carefully.

The dungeon was dark and cold. It smelled of rotting limestone and dust. Queen Cleona had assured them that if they went straight through, they would find the way out, but Ava was determined to check every cell for her prince. The others followed as she crept quietly along the dirty floor and peered into the locked chambers one by one. Many were empty, a few were not.

They were able to skirt by unseen until something in an open cell caught Ava' eye. She darted inside and took it from the ground. It was Alucio's necklace—she knew it right away. It was a chain of silver. The pendant was the emblem of Dread Kingdom and bore the mark of loyalty to the king. Ava had seen it around Alucio's neck when they met. He'd explained to her that he never took it off. Her breath stilled as she pressed it to her chest.

"What is it?" Cosette asked. She and Simone gathered around their friend and saw the chain that wrapped her fist.

"He must have been here," Ava breathed. She then slowly opened her hand and showed it to them. "It belongs to Alucio."

Simone felt ill. "What does this mean? If he was here and he is no longer... What have they done with him?" She was afraid to know the answer. All of them were.

Ava's eyes began to burn of tears, her soul to fill with heartache.

"They've done nothing with him," a deep familiar voice spoke from behind them.

They turned to see John and another burly guard towering over them. They resisted the urge to call him by name since he was not alone. They didn't know if the other guard could be trusted.

Ava however, was concerned only with one thing. "You know of the prince? Where is he then?!" she shouted. "Where is he?" She rushed toward the guard who had spoken and grabbed his jacket forcefully. Cosette and Simone tried to stop her, but to no avail. "Tell me what you know, or else suffer a most heinous death," she warned the big man.

John was taken aback. "You know the prince of Dread? Then you are spies," he remarked.

The women were caught off guard and the men began to push them back into the cell. "Get in here, you charlatans. Ethan will hear about this!" the larger man blasted.

Ava struggled with him as he twisted her arm. He was enraged by her impudence and slammed her into the stone wall. "Take that! I'm always getting lip from you women! And it always comes to this!" He then kicked her to the ground. "I always have to teach you a lesson!"

As Ava's lip bled, she recovered to her feet. Her eyes narrowed and before he knew it, she quickly snatched the dagger from her garter and shoved it into his gut. With great malice, she removed it and stuck him again. "And so begins your heinous death, you frothing filth!"

Ava held on to the dagger as he slid to the floor, her eyes locked with his until his sight was no more. She then retrieved her knife and wiped it with his tunic.

She turned to see Cosette and Simone held their knives to John's neck. This had been why he hadn't interfered with the struggle. Once he was calm, they removed the knives and hid them once more. He was stunned by their prowess, but more so that they seemed to be letting him go.

Cosette spoke to him calmly. "We mean you no harm, but we could not let you restrain us," she said.

He still seemed a bit unnerved. Cosette tried to calm him. "We are not spies. We came here of our own will and without permission. We have come to stop Ethan."

John was shocked, but not as shocked as the women had expected. "I knew it was something of the sort," he told them. "You were different. I saw the kindness in your eyes when you looked at me and at each other, and I felt the underlying disdain when you looked at Ethan. He is blind to it, but I knew it because I feel that same contempt for him."

The women were relieved to know the truth. "Then why do you serve him?"

"Because he keeps my true love alive. Long ago, he discovered us together and asked her to choose him or me. She went with him. That's when he locked her in the tower. I know she doesn't love me anymore, but I feel that he keeps her alive to torture me and if I leave him, he would have no reason to keep her alive."

He was visibly saddened. Cosette took his hand. "It is Queen Cleona," she said.

His eyes quickly met hers. "How could you know? He killed everyone who knew and ran off the others before they found out!"

Cosette slipped the tied locks of red hair from her pocket and slipped it into his hand. "She loves you still."

John was overcome. He saw the hair. He heard Cosette's words, but felt as if in a dream.

"Go to her," said Simone. "Rescue her, this will be your only chance."

Ava gently moved the women to the side and moved to face John. "First, what of my Alucio? You must tell me what you know!"

"You love him, don't you?" John asked. He also knew the look of genuine affection.

"Tell me, please," she said. "I must know."

"I haven't seen him. I swear it on my love's own life," said John. "The necklace was found on the ground next to another man. Before we grabbed him, he put the necklace on. He must have left it behind for some reason or it was taken off."

"Where is this prisoner now?" Ava asked.

John stared intently. "Ethan doesn't keep prisoners for long."

The women knew this meant he was no longer available for questioning.

John continued. "Be warned: Ethan means to move on Dread Kingdom by dawn. But now he looks for you. It has delayed his plans as he is now sure you are infiltrators. He has demanded we find you. The guards now scour the grounds in search of nothing else."

"Go to Cleona," said Cosette. "We will take care of Ethan."

"But how?" asked John.

"Never you mind such things," said Ava, repeating the words he'd spoken to them earlier in the night. "But it will be done. Now we must go."

They pointed John the way of the passages and prepared for the hunt. It was time for this battle to end. Ethan was going to find them all right, and he wouldn't live to regret it.

# Chapter Sixteen

Dawn was approaching as the moon was slowly but surely making her descent. Ava, Cosette, and Simone had searched the castle for Ethan but it was empty. Every man was out in the fields and hills preparing for battle. All but the three they saw searching for them on the grounds—three that looked just about their sizes. The women would have to get into Ethan's camp, but not so straightforwardly as before. They would need to be cunning, careful, and unnoticed.

They sneaked outside and around a dark corner of the castle where the young men stood sharing a pipe, obviously breaking from their search. The women then ambushed them. The men never stood a chance. They'd sent Simone in seemingly alone with her dress loosened seductively while the other two women attacked from behind. After knocking them all unconscious, the women borrowed their tunics, pants, riding boots, and swords.

Mistress Dorothea sat in a chair next to her king's bedside. He showed color, and was warm but not hot. This pleased her to no end as she felt he was finally making a serious turn for the better. She listened for even the slightest sound nearing his chambers, yet there were none. She didn't trust the stranger who had come so many hours earlier and wouldn't announce himself. She knew it was a spy, that's why she'd lied to him about the king having been up drinking. But she was anxious over the fact that she couldn't leave to alert anyone, and there was no sign of Alucio's return. The moon was setting and Dorothea felt something was brewing in the air this morning. She knew there was trouble afoot and hoped for some bit of good news.

King Dominicus began to move. The old woman stood and took his hand. She was eager for him to awaken. He turned his head her way but stopped moving. Her hope began to fade, but suddenly he opened his eyes.

"My king!" she exclaimed quietly, while holding his hand.

His head remained still, but his narrow eyes scanned the room. "Where are Queen Geneva's servants?" he asked.

"Well—" said Dorothea. She wasn't quite sure where to begin. But as she hesitated, she saw the king's brow tighten and heard a deep rumble from within his chest. "Please don't be upset, Your Majesty, they left this note—"

The three servants tucked the black tunics in to their fitted pants and strapped on their new belts and sheathed swords. Ava wore Alucio's necklace around her neck and the three women mounted the guards' horses and stole into the woods in search of Ethan's camp.

Once they reached a high point above the valley, they could see the tents of the camp among the trees. They also knew there were many guards hidden sporadically throughout the woods preparing for the mêlée, but they could slip past them unnoticed. It was Ethan they wanted. It was there they left the horses and decided to tread the rest of the path on foot. They took to the brush and trees instead of the road as not to leave any footprints. They crept through the brush unheard and unseen. The light of the sun was beginning to add color to the dark morning sky. Soon Ethan's men would storm Dread Kingdom to an unknown end, in hopes of conquering the castle of the ailing king. Ethan must be stopped before it was too late.

But just as the woman approached the camp, the evil Prince emerged from his tent and the horns began to blow, signaling the beginning of combat. The women wanted to rush him, but didn't know what to do. The men took to their horses, and, to the servants' tremendous surprise, what seemed like thousands of men came pouring out of the forest and heading for the border of Dread.

"It's beginning!" Simone yelled.

Over the shouts of the men and gallops of the horses, the servants were able to speak freely. The sun began to show brightly across the land.

"What shall we do now?" Simone shouted. "Prince Alucio is gone, and the king lies dying. Dread will be defeated!"

Ava turned and grabbed her shoulder. "Not today!" she screamed.

Ava then ran back to the horses. Cosette and Simone followed fast behind. Once they arrived, Cosette and Ava took the lead as they exploded into the sea of men, running unnoticed alongside them as they rode hard into the kingdom of Dread. The faction was met with the swords and spears of the feared Dread Knights. They were a fierce and ominous group, but they also seemed surprised by the immense size of Ethan's army. He had unknowingly taken over the smaller kingdoms to the east and west of Aldren and now used their armies against the kingdom of Dread.

Though Ethan's men outnumbered the Dread knights, the battle was equally fought. But they could only hold for so long. The Dread knights were slowly being pushed backward and closer to the castle. Simone's frailty had long passed, and she and her cohorts began to engage in the fighting themselves. As they fought to protect themselves, they found that adrenaline mixed with profound purpose was a great teacher as to the ways of the sword. They fought their way closer to Ethan. He was often displaced in the sea of men, but the women never lost sight.

They worked their way toward him and his eyes never lay upon their presence. As the battle raged closer to the castle, many of the men now fought on foot. The servants leaped from their horses and clashing steel against steel made their way to Ethan's side. He finally saw them and the severity in their eyes. He suddenly knew their purpose was ill. He yelled, "You've made it this far? And just to die at my own hand!"

Ava pulled the necklace into view and held tight to it. He saw this and his lips curved wickedly. "So," he spat, "You are loyal to King Dominicus. I will kill you just like I killed the last man who wore that necklace."

Ava thought he was referring to Prince Alucio and raised her sword. But Simone quickly charged against him and stabbed him in the stomach. Cosette and Ava stepped back as Ethan dropped to one knee. Then, Cosette struck him across the jaw with the pummel of her sword. Blood flew from his lips as he fell to the ground.

Ethan's men however seemed to be overpowering the Dread Knights when suddenly from the gates of the castle a dark horse appeared. It was the king charging into the battle. The great king had risen. His hair flowed like the wind and he rode like a firestorm taking out droves of men in his wake. He was soon followed by Sir Erec and Sir Lazander. They tore into Ethan's men.

The number of Dread Knights was still waning until a new and obvious rumble began to quake the ground. The entire barrage of knights and guards was forced to take notice as a massive army came pouring over the hills in the east. They were the soldiers of Geneva's army led by two charging figures on enormous steeds—one in gilded armor.

Ethan began to clamber to his feet as the women were engaged in battle around him. They were beaten and bruised but would fight as strong or better than any man. They would not go down without a valiant effort.

Ava saw Ethan as he came at her with his sword and sliced her arm with the tip. He then knocked her down with a swift backhand. She stammered, but to his astonishment quickly rose to her feet. "Next time, you'd better keep me down," she warned.

He then made another attempt at her but she stabbed him through until the hilt would go no further. She then grabbed him as he fell. "Before you die, tell me what you have done with Prince Alucio!" she yelled.

He smiled wickedly but it was too late, after a few moments he was no more. Her answer however came in the form of a deep and booming voice. "I am here!" Alucio yelled, as he swooped her up onto his horse while racing by. The other servants caught up with Lazander and Erec and rode with them out of the battle and into the safety of the Dread castle's walls.

The armies of Queen Geneva and the king of Dread cleared the realm of every one of Ethan's assembly. There were many who immediately surrendered after Ethan's death and pleaded for their lives as Ethan had forced them to comply with his rule. Some were spared and able to return to their families.

At the battle's end, the soldier in gilded armor approached King Dominicus at the castle gates. They dismounted their horses. Dominicus removed his chest armor and was bandaged beneath his loose tunic, his eyes showed what he had been through, but still managed to pierce through to the soul of his companion. He held his ribs with his left arm and with his right removed the helmet from Geneva's head. He drank her in only for a moment. Then he pulled her close and took her mouth into his in front of his entire guard. Their love would be a secret no more.

Prince Alucio had simply been away, not missing. He'd made the long journey to Queen Geneva's castle to plead for her assistance in the battle. But he didn't have to utter a word. When the queen received word that the feared prince had entered her kingdom, she immediately summoned her army. She knew what his presence meant. What's more, as she spoke to Alucio, she prepared herself for battle as well. She would ride alongside her lover's brother, leading her men straight into the wages of war. She would fight to support Dread Kingdom, to avenge the offenses made against the great king.

Side by side they rode into Dread thrashing sword and spear against their adversaries when suddenly they saw the three servants submerged in the throes of the chaotic battle. At once they knew things were more than they seemed. Alucio immediately bolted and retrieved his beloved Ava, and when the battle came to a close, Queen Geneva made way to the amorous arms of her cherished king.

Prince Alucio rode his horse to a rear-side entrance to the castle. There, he assisted Ava off of the dark steed and gently pressed her against the wall. Her lips were silent, but her eyes spoke for her heart. She was in love with the fearsome man before her, and though many thought him dead, she'd refused to stop searching for him—no matter the cost.

Now, her heart was at peace. To have him here, alive, standing tall and stronger than ever, his fierce eyes berated every inch of her body, the intoxicating musk of him filled her with such elation that all recent memories eluded her. But now, in his line of sight, in his royal presence, she knew she must answer for betraying his orders to watch over the king. She must admit to leading a rebellion across the borders of the kingdom and into the enemy's own hands.

She stood there, frozen and wordless as his eyes washed over her own. His hand neared her neck and she breathed sharply. But his fingers dipped into the top of her borrowed tunic and pulled out the heavy silver necklace. Alucio looked at it, his mind all at once filled with knowing, when suddenly he dropped the thing and kissed her.

She was surprised but hungry for him. She kissed him back more fervently than before. His mouth was pleasing—his kiss was inviting and true. He was not dead. This moment was real. Every emotion she'd felt since he'd disappeared collided with every feeling of lust and love she'd felt for him since they'd met.

They, along with their friends, and even more so, the great king and queen, had discovered that the moments in love were the most precious, and since there was no telling how few they might be, not a single moment should be wasted again.

Several nights later, a great celebration was prepared in Dread Castle's Spirit Hall. It was largely in honor of Queen Geneva's three brave servants, but also the victory over Prince Ethan, and the alliance of the three greatest kingdoms of the realm.

Gowns were brought to the three servants' rooms. They were bathed, dressed and made up as royalty from their hair and lips down to their jewel-encrusted shoes. Each was a gift from King Dominicus who'd also given them the most extravagant jewelry they had ever laid eyes upon. The three scarcely recognized themselves or each other when they met in the foyer with their appointed maids. They had never been waited on before, and were speechless when the women curtsied and bowed.

"You are absolutely breathtaking, both of you," Ava said to her friends. Her eyes were wet with tears.

"So are you," said Simone and Cosette.

Cosette inhaled deeply. "Do you suppose this is all a dream?"

"If it is," said Simone, "I hope we never wake from it."

They smiled and hugged each other tightly. It was almost time. Suddenly, three unfamiliar but handsome Dread knights appeared and offered their arms to the women. "This way ladies. Your presence is anxiously awaited."

Ava, Cosette, and Simone walked with the men and tried to look as comfortable in their new clothes as possible. The men escorted them to two very large engraved wooden doors. Two guards opened them at once, and before they could be announced the crowd gasped at their great beauty and began to mumble in awe. The king stood slowly. He could not believe his eyes. Queen Geneva also stood and smiled with approval.

The women were announced and trumpets were played as they walked the long, carpeted, path to the king. Sir Lazander and Sir Erec smiled proudly. They stood firmly beside the king and queen. Prince Alucio however took two steps down toward Ava but King Dominicus held his arm out and stopped him. "Wait," he commanded. "There is a matter of great importance that must first be addressed."

The women, now having reached the foot of Dominicus' stair, did not simply curtsy, but knelt before him. Their escorts stood aside and bowed to the king.

Dominicus spoke firmly as the women remained kneeling, and he began to draw the sword from the sheath at his hip. "The three of you have demonstrated willfulness and disobedience. You have given yourselves unto a mutinous duty, a treasonable plot against a royal figure, and contravened the direct orders of the prince of Dread—a task that alone commands a penalty of death."

The king took a deliberate and lengthy pause and allowed the servants to absorb all that he had said. He then continued. "And you did all of this at terrific risk to your own lives, in attempt to preserve the lives of my brother and of myself."

The women's eyes slowly lifted from the ground and rose toward the king who suddenly spoke more warmly.

"You have shown great bravery, equal to or greater than even the bravest of knights. You have given to this dark king something that cannot be bought, or crafted, or dreamed. You have bestowed upon this kingdom the gift of light in our dark hours. For that, I am indebted to you and eternally grateful." His voice began to rise so that all could hear and he raised his sword.

"Let it be known throughout the land, I, King Dominicus of Dread Kingdom, do now bestow upon these women an honor equivalent to the appointment of knighthood. From this day forward you shall each carry the title of Lady of the Order of Imperial Knights." He lowered his sword and gave each her name. The reflective metal sparkled in their astonished eyes.

He then made them rise and Geneva pinned on each of them a golden broach that matched Alucio's silver necklace. It was the symbol of loyalty to the kingdom of Dread. Queen Geneva smiled kindly at her former servants as Dominicus looked on. "You have been quite busy, haven't you?" she asked.

They each parted their lips to speak, but she hushed them and continued softly. "What you have done for the great king, you have done for me as well."

The women knew she spoke of her love for the king and what might have happened.

"I have always known the three of you were special. But your profound bravery and headship in the shadows of these inexplicable days has amazed even your shrewd queen. For this I am proud, but even more—I too am eternally grateful. First, from this day forward, you will be servant to no man—or woman. And second, as a minute token of my gratitude I give each of you a ring that has been passed down in my family for ages."

The queen took each lady by the right hand and slipped on her finger a gold ring emblazoned with a fine and rare gem of incredible size. For Simone, serendibite; for Cosette, crimson red diamond; and for Ava, jadeite.

The servants were aghast at this gesture and knelt before the generous queen and once more before the king. They thanked them for bestowing such incredible generosity upon them.

Ava stepped forward to face her queen. "Your Highness, I know I speak for the three of us when I say that words could not express my tremendous gratitude for all that you have given me in all my days in your kingdom. It has been my extreme pleasure to serve you." She then looked into the eyes of the king and again curtsied him. "And, Your Royal Majesty, I am truly humbled by your benevolence, and consumed with infinite gratitude for your munificence. You are truly a magnificent king, and I would gladly risk my life for you again without a moment's thought. Anything you ask of me I shall eagerly oblige."

She then bowed her head and Dominicus took a step closer and lifted her chin with his fingertips. "Anything? I am glad to hear of it."

Ava looked at him blankly.

"I would have you marry my brother," he said.

Ava did not speak. She was winded by this statement. She took a deep breath of air and her eyes immediately met with those of the prince who descended the stairs.

King Dominicus took her hand and placed it in the palm of the prince.

Alucio knelt before her as if she was royalty rather than he. His dark brown tresses draped each shoulder of his long velvet coat. His broad chest shone through the loose tunic, the silver emblem shining bright. "Will you be my wife, Lady Ava?" His voice was pleading and loving.

"Nothing could fill my life with greater pleasure," she replied.

The queen and king were first to embrace them, followed by a jubilant Cosette and Simone.

The crowd in attendance was thrilled at all of the news this glorious night, but there was more to come. The horns began to sound and the crowd parted for the entrance of Queen Cleona and the newly crowned Prince John.

# Chapter Seventeen

The beautiful Queen Cleona had been restored to her crown, and appeared in the hall even more radiant than anyone had ever seen her. She held the arm of the new and humble Prince John, who was dashing in his regal new form. Together they lit up the hall. Their ardor was evident to all who laid eyes on them.

A grand feast took place that night, and the castle was alive with music, dancing, and laughter. But later in the evening, a gathering took place in a private setting. Present were King Dominicus and Queen Geneva, the newly knighted ladies, Prince Alucio, Queen Cleona and Prince John.

King Dominicus spoke first in his usual dark and serious tone. "In what is merely an afternoon, plans have been finalized that were set in motion long ago. Queen Geneva and I have shared an alliance for many years, and have decided to forge our sovereignty into one vast empire. We will call the realm Imlad en Galad Mor, the Valley of Light and Dark. A palace shall be constructed at the highest point in the region which is also the center-most point. And there we shall live together as husband and wife—King and Queen of Galad Mor."

The former servants were quiet, but their astonished and elated eyes were apparent to their astute queen.

"Many congratulations are in order, King Dominicus," said Queen Cleona. "The dark king seems to have met his match. It is absolutely splendid news," she stated sincerely.

Once everyone had shared their pleasantries, Dominicus continued. "At one corner of this new territory is Geneva's castle. Her daughter, Princess Nadia and Nadia's husband, Prince Francis of

Carrollton, will return from that far away land to be custodians of the castle.

My brother, the prince of Dread will be ruler of this castle and the surrounding kingdom. He will be supreme ruler, second only to me."

Dominicus gripped his brother's shoulder. "You shall be king of this realm when my days are over. But I want you to share in this now while I am still alive. My brother, ruler of Dread Kingdom—and the most feared ruler in all the land." Dominicus smiled.

Alucio was humored. "I think that title will belong to you for the rest of your days, my brother."

Queen Cleona then stood to make her announcement in turn. It was an announcement that King Dominicus and Queen Geneva were aware of.

Her gaze met with Ladies Cosette and Simone. "As you now know, Ethan took control of the small kingdoms to the east and west of my own Aldren. They are now left without rule. Prince John and I require stewards to live in the castles of those kingdoms—stewards who will oversee the needs of the villagers, act as council, and ultimately keep rule over those kingdoms in our absence. Ethan has left my kingdom in a shambles, and we have a lot of toil ahead to restore Aldren to its former glory. You have shown extraordinary courage, headship, virtue, and integrity. These are the qualities a kingdom requires in a steward. We ask that you, Lady Simone accept the duty of steward of the kingdom of Gree, and you, Lady Cosette of the kingdom of Annon. You do not have to decide tonight."

"Why, yes of course," said Cosette, and Simone agreed as well. "We do not require any more time to consider it. It would be our honor and privilege."

Cosette wondered silently how she could get word to Lady Hilda....

The following months were busy but joyous. The women had settled comfortably into their new lives, and as the cool breeze of late autumn moved in from the low lands, the royals celebrated three grand ceremonies. First and second, the marriages of King Dominicus to Queen Geneva and of Prince Alucio to Lady Ava.

The third was the return of Princess Nadia and Prince Francis. Indeed, the realm had never been so sated with jollity and merriment.

The new palace had begun to make its glorious appearance. Dorothea, through diligent attention to detail, had single-handedly discovered the true emissary to Ethan's army. It was a cook who'd been replaced by Cosette in the king's time of need. Dorothea handed him over to the king and was subsequently offered the chance to retire from her duties with gratitude. She was given her own manor house overlooking the beautiful river. She was urged to retire peacefully and to never lift another finger of service—but she wouldn't hear of it. She insisted on continuing her service to the king, and so was appointed as head nursemaid of Prince Alucio's children, the first of whom was on his way.

# Also by Maria Christine...

## Her Eternal Love

A dark and romantic fantasy tale set in the Realm
of Shadows, where you'll find supernatural,
immortal, and sinister beings. Yet, even here, the
bonds of blood are strong and love is eternal.

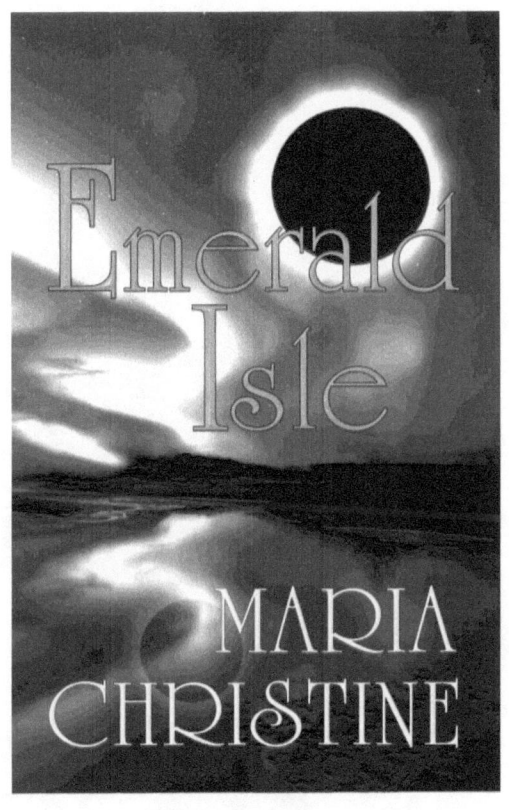

### Emerald Isle

A modern Gothic folktale & paranormal romance
set in Ireland. Miranda Kelly is in love. But legend
tells of a supernatural danger that nears, and the
man who has stolen her heart may be bound to
this legend in more ways than one.

# For more

about these and other titles,
visit www.MariaChristineOnline.com
and www.NocturnaPress.com